THE PROFESSOR'S OBSESSION

EMMA BRAY

Chapter One

Poppy

"No way," I shake my head firmly at my best friend, but she continues to nod hers in contradiction, a huge grin on her face.

"We totally can't do that, Melissa. It's crazy!"

"Yes way," she says with even more conviction than I used.

"But why would you even want to? You certainly don't need the money," I point out to her.

She shrugs. "I get off on the thrill. So sue me."

I frown. Melissa and I've been best friends ever since I was placed in this crummy town by the system.

We're as different as two girls can be. Whereas I have wavy, dark brown hair and a slim frame, Melissa is a blonde bombshell with curves guys would kill for. Whereas I'm a foster kid with nothing, she's a rich girl with everything.

I don't know what caused her to take up with me so much, but I'm glad she did. The first day in a new high school is always rough, but instead of being a snotty rich girl like so many at the other schools I attended, she was kind.

We were assigned together as lab partners, and we just hit it off somehow.

Melissa's my best friend. Actually, she's my only friend. I've been shuffled around so much it's been hard to put down roots or stay in touch with anyone long enough to develop a meaningful friendship.

"This way you can go to college with me, and we can be roomies!" she practically squeals.

College. Sure, I've applied, but it was to shut her up more than anything. And maybe a tiny part of me just wants to know if I'm good enough to get accepted.

I always knew there was no way I'll go, though.

I can't afford it.

And I don't want to be one of those people who takes out huge loans and starts out in debt. No way.

College just isn't for people like me. Rejects of the system.

I'm not bitter about it. It is what it is.

It's all I can do to make ends meet to pay for this crummy apartment. Like, seriously, the paint is peeling off the walls, and it's super tiny, but at least I have a roof over my head. The day I turned eighteen, I was officially out of the system—not that there's much love lost between me and my latest foster parents. They weren't overly cruel, but they certainly weren't wanting to keep me forever. I've had worse ones.

They were even nice enough to hook me up with this job. I wait tables in the diner out front in exchange for a meager wage, a few tips, and this shoddy room in the back of the place. The place is definitely a dump, but at least I'm not on the streets like so many other orphans when they come of age.

It might not be much, but that doesn't mean I'm desperate enough to do what Melissa's proposing.

"There's no way I'm giving up my virginity for money."

"Don't think of it that way," Melissa says instantly. "Think of it as trading it in for a better life."

I roll my eyes at her. "Yeah, because that sounds so much better."

"Come on, Poppy." Her blue eyes plead with me. "You don't want to live like this forever, do you? You *need* to come with me to college. You're way smarter than me. You're meant for great things. I know it." She says it with such conviction, and that's one of the things I love about my best friend the most. She doesn't care where I come from. She truly believes in me.

"You said money is the issue," she adds. "This will solve all that. Not only will this one sacrifice pay for school, but you can move out of this..." she pauses, her eyes sweeping over the crummy room, trying to come up with a word that won't offend me, until she settles with, "place."

"How much money are we talking?" I ask her begrudgingly. It doesn't mean I'm seriously considering it.

Because I'm not.

Right?

It's crazy.

It's wrong.

It's debasing.

It's...

Melissa's eyes shine with hope as she drops the number on me.

My eyes about bug out of my head.

What did she say?

Good lord. That kind of cash would be enough to go to college ten times if I wanted to. Or to just not go to college. To just start a new life.

She laughs at my shocked expression. "See? We *have* to do this."

I shake my head, trying to clear it. I understand why she'd suggest it to me since I'm basically penniless, but her parents are loaded, so I still don't get why she would even consider it.

"I still don't get why *you* want to do this," I tell her pointedly.

She shrugs again. "I told you. I'm a thrill-seeker. Plus, it'd be nice to have some money that's all mine."

I can see that. Melissa has always been more the one to walk on the wild side, while I'm the more cautious friend. She's fearless. And while her parents are loaded, she hates having to ask them for everything. I certainly understand wanting to be independent.

"Where did you even hear about a place like this?" I ask her.

She smiles impishly. "I have my sources."

"Still," I say slowly, "the thought of giving it up to some creepy old man..." I trail off, shuddering.

"Look," Melissa levels a frank stare at me. "It's

the one thing we have of value that we can control. Most girls lose it in the back of a car to a fumbling boy. No one ever talks about their first time being good. I mean. Ever. I've heard enough to know," she adds knowingly. "So why shouldn't we at least get something out of it?"

Before I can say anything, she rushes to add, "Plus, this place is like legit. It's the real deal. The guys who go here are loaded, and you put down what you're okay with."

My brows furrow, "What we're okay with?'

"Yeah, like if you're down for more than vanilla."

I about choke on my water, and Melissa laughs.

"We'll automatically get bigs bucks just for being virgins," she states matter-of-factly, "so anything extra would just be extra cash for extra kink."

No thanks. I'm not greedy. Or kinky. I don't think. Actually, I don't really know anything about sex other than the basics. I've never even been kissed.

"What about waiting for love and all that jazz?" I point out to her.

She scoffs. "Puh-lease. Life's not a fairytale," she states frankly. "You of all people should know that."

I could be offended, but I know she doesn't mean it the way it sounds. Melissa's just brutally honest. Another one of the things I love about her. She doesn't sugarcoat anything. She gives it to you straight.

And she's right. I do know. Life isn't a fairytale.

"You've got a point there," I concede.

She nods solemnly. "But life could sure as hell be a lot better if we had loaded bank accounts," she adds.

I can't help the laugh that escapes me, and Melissa grins triumphantly, knowing she's got me. "So you down?" she asks.

I allow myself to imagine actually doing this. One night. If I can get through one night, my life could change forever. I could be roomies with Melissa. I could have the normal life other students have.

"I guess it wouldn't hurt to check it out," I concede.

She throws her arms around me and squeals.

———

Brad

I hate surprises.

I fucking hate them.

I glare at my old college buddies. They know that too.

I agreed to go out with them for drinks for old times' sake. It's not often the four of us are all in town.

I'm not gullible by any means. That's why it's even more incredible they've managed to so royally set me up.

It's my thirtieth birthday. That right there should have been enough to make me suspicious. What are the odds that all three of them just so happen to be in town on my birthday of all days?

I should have known they were up to something. None of them are married, and apparently none of them have grown the fuck up yet. They still party like the frat boys we used to be. Not that I've ever been as big into the partying scene as they are.

I've always been more focused on my classes. I wanted to make something of myself. Now, I focus on my career. Once I made my mark in the world of art, I decided to teach it. I'm a professor at NYU, and I should be prepping for the upcoming semester—not fucking off with these boneheads.

We have a a private room at one of the swankiest bars in the city where we've been throwing back scotch. At least they've graduated from their beer hat days.

It's honestly been nice catching up with the guys.

Steve works in tech. Johnny's at Wall Street, and Eric's…well, Eric's Eric.

He comes from money and can do what he wants to do. Which is apparently a whole lot of nothing. The guy lives life to the fullest. I'll give him that.

And I'd bet my left nut this is all his idea.

Steve and Johnny have already ducked out on some bullshit calls they suddenly had to take, and that leaves me with Eric.

I narrow my eyes at my old college buddy. "What did you do, Eric?"

He just laughs, unfazed by the warning in my tone. "Look, man, you never do anything but work. You're so uptight and tense all the time. How long's it been since you've gotten laid?"

"That's none of your goddamn business," I snap at him, not liking where this is going.

He only laughs harder, and I think about cold-cocking him like I used to do back when we lived in the frat house together.

"That long, huh?" his mouth quirks up in a grin.

I run a hand over my face, frustrated beyond belief with this whole conversation, "Eric, if you've hired a stripper to come in here as some sort of sick birthday present, so help me God…"

He cuts me off with, "She's not a stripper. She's an escort."

"Jesus Christ," I mutter as I start to stand. I am *not* in the mood for this shit.

Eric puts a hand out like he's going to hold me back, but he drops his hand when he sees what I'm sure is a murderous look in my eyes.

"It's not what you think, man. This place is top-dollar. You get what I'm saying?" he asks me conspiratorially.

I glare at him. "I don't have to pay for pussy," I growl.

Eric shrugs. "So don't fuck her. Or do. Whatever. Just enjoy the company of a beautiful woman for one night."

I don't know who the hell he thinks he is, but he's definitely overstepping the bounds of our friendship. Just as I'm getting ready to tell him that, there's a faint knock at the door.

Eric grins wickedly at me before going over to open the door. "Happy birthday," he calls over his shoulder at me before exiting the room, leaving a woman standing in the shadows of the doorway.

"God fucking damn it," I mutter, preparing myself to tell her this has all been a mistake and that her services won't be needed, but then she steps hesitantly into the room before closing the door behind her. She turns around and steps slowly into the light, long waves of deep brown hair falling over her shoulders and down her back. She raises her downcast head, and I feel like the breath's been knocked out of me.

An angel. She's a fucking angel.

Big, doe-brown eyes look up at me with all the innocence in the world. That's what she looks like too. A little deer caught in the headlights. Her eyes are wide, and her puffy pink lips fall slightly open in a gasp as my eyes meet hers.

"You're not a creepy old man," she says breathily before her hands come up to cover her mouth as if she can't believe what she just said. Pink stains her cheeks, and I can't help the quirk that tips up the side of my lips.

"I hope not," I tell her, trying to set her at ease. Her nervousness is a palpable thing that can almost be seen in the dim lighting of the private room.

Against my better judgement, my eyes sweep over her body. God, she's tiny. Just a slip of a thing, slim and girlish, yet utterly feminine with just enough curves in all the right places. The white dress she's wearing drapes softly off her shoulders and then flares out at her hips before falling gently against her thighs. Despite her short stature, somehow her legs seem to go on forever, maybe due in part to the little white stilettos she's wearing.

Despite my resolve, I feel my cock react, lengthening in my pants. Sinful innocence. That's what she is.

I've seen strippers and escorts before, but none of them ever looked like this. They were always older than their years with haunted looks in their eyes. Nothing like this young, innocent-looking little thing.

She looks too pure to touch. So what the hell is she doing working for an escort service?

"How old are you, sweetheart?" I ask her.

She wrings her hands nervously as she answers, "Eighteen."

I close my eyes, hating myself that my cock gets even harder at the way she voices her age but also thanking whatever god is out there that she's legal.

Wait, what the fuck am I thinking?

There's no way I'm actually going to have sex with this girl—no matter that she looks ten times more perfect than my most perfect fantasy.

I'm a college professor for Christ's sake. I'm supposed to be a good example, a role model.

I don't pay for pussy. I didn't ask for this. Eric and his meddling ass...

I must be scowling because she looks even more nervous than she did a moment before. "Is that a problem?" Her voice shakes as she asks the question.

I run a hand over my face again as I croak out a dry, humorless laugh. "No, sweetheart. That's not it."

"Oh." Her shoulders fall, and she wraps her arms about herself protectively. "I'm not what you were looking for," she says dejectedly.

I stare at her. Is she fucking serious? Does she not realize how beautiful she is?

I take a step toward her, but then I stop, not trusting myself to touch her. "You're gorgeous."

She peeks up at me from lowered lashes, shyly, and God help me, but I can't help imagining what it would be like to see her looking up at me like that with her sweet lips wrapped around my cock.

Fuck, maybe Eric's right. Maybe it has been too long since I've gotten laid.

As soon as I think it, though, I know it's more than that.

This girl…there's something about her. I've seen my share of beautiful women, but no one has ever stirred up the sensations she's stirring up in me just by looking up at me so shyly.

I've never reacted so strongly to any woman

before. I don't know what it is about this girl, but I want to claim her, mark her as mine and only mine.

"What's your name?" I ask her, dying to know anything about her.

"Poppy," she answers, still wringing her hands together nervously. *Poppy.* It suits her. Sweet and pretty, just like her.

"I'm Brad," I tell her.

"Brad," she repeats softly, and I have to bite back a groan as my cock twitches at just the sound of my name coming from her lips. How can just my name in her sweet little voice fill me with such lust?

My eyes dart down to her little fingers. "Relax, Poppy," I tell her, liking the taste of her name on my tongue.

"I'm sorry," she whispers, her face flushing. "I've never done this before."

I've already guessed that just by her nervousness, but hearing her confirm it gives me an inexplicable sense of relief. I don't like the thought of her being an escort and letting guys paw at her.

"Why are you?" I ask her.

Her brow furrows. "What?"

"Why are you doing this?" I repeat my question patiently.

"Oh," her cheeks heat even further before she mumbles, "I need the money."

I frown. "You're not in any sort of trouble, are you? No one's forcing you to do this?" Just the thought of her being forced into something like this makes my blood curdle with fury.

She shakes her head, setting her brown locks bouncing prettily. *Jesus.* "No, it's my choice."

When I don't say anything, she starts rambling, "Well, it was my bestie's idea. She said our virginity is the one thing of value we have and since most girls have such a horrible first time anyway, we might as well be compensated for it."

She looks up at me with wide eyes and then claps her hands over her entire face this time, shielding her pink cheeks from my gaze. "Oh god, I can't believe I said that. I'm probably screwing this up so bad. I'm sorry. I'm sorry."

She shakes her head again, but all I can do is stand there in shock. *Christ.* A virgin. She's a fucking virgin. And she's handing herself over to the highest bidder.

My jaw hardens as I think of some of the sick fucks she could have ended up with. Old perverts who get off on deflowering virgins.

I don't have that kind of fetish, but Christ if the

thought that I could be *this* girl's one and only doesn't make me hard as a motherfucker.

I take a deep breath to try to banish those thoughts from my head. This angel deserves better than this. She doesn't deserve to lose her virginity in some private room in a bar to a stranger.

"It's okay, Poppy," I tell her. "You don't have to do anything."

Chapter Two

Poppy

I can't help the tears that prick my eyes as he tells me I don't have to do anything.

Oh god, I should be relieved, shouldn't I? I've been nervous about this all day. I almost chickened out at the last minute. He's giving me an easy way out.

Why am I filled with nothing but disappointment?

I look up at the Adonis standing before me. He's nothing like the old man I expected. He's tall and muscular and incredibly good-looking. He's wearing jeans and a T-shirt that fits over his muscles like a second skin. He looks like he just walked off the cover of a GQ magazine with his dark hair that flows back from his face in casual waves. His eyes are an electric blue that makes my toes curl when his gaze lands on me.

He told me I was gorgeous, but I know now that he was just being nice to me. *He's* the one who's gorgeous.

No wonder he doesn't want me. He's probably used to blonde bombshells like Melissa.

"I'm so sorry," I apologize to him again.

He frowns at me before he finally reaches out and tips my chin up to look at him. "Stop apologizing," he tells me. "You have nothing to be sorry for."

"But I ruined your birthday," I whisper, the humiliation making me want a hole to just open up and swallow me right now.

He laughs, and I feel my face flaming even more, the sting of rejection hurting.

But that sting quickly morphs into something else. Anger.

Dammit, I didn't psyche myself up for this only to back out now. I need that money for a new life. Now that I've talked myself into this, I'm not backing out now. I have to try.

He paid for me, so he obviously wants sex. So

that's what I need to do. Be sexy. No wonder he doesn't want me. I've been acting like a scared little girl.

Mustering up all the courage I can, I take a deep breath, stand up on my tip-toes and pull his head down to me, pressing my lips against his to take my first kiss.

And it's nothing like I could have ever imagined. The moment my lips touch his, it's like a trigger has been pulled. His big arms are suddenly around me, hauling my body flush up against him. I feel his hardness pressing up against my stomach, and it makes me tremble.

One of his hands moves up to cup my face, angling it up toward him. I feel his tongue sliding against the seam of my lips, and I gasp in surprise. My gasp only gives him an opening to slip his tongue into my mouth.

I'm not prepared for the electricity that shoots through me, making my legs go weak. Thank God, he still has one arm wrapped around my waist, or I think I'd have sunk straight to the floor.

I've never had alcohol before, but I know that's what he tastes like. Alcohol and fresh mint and something else that's just entirely him.

His tongue meets mine, dancing against it, and he

lets out a groan that rocks me to my core. My stomach clenches at the sound, and I feel wetness pool between my legs.

"So fucking sweet," he whispers against my lips before he trails kisses and licks and nips down my throat, sending tingles down my spine.

Suddenly, he lifts me up, and my arms and legs wrap around him instinctively. His hardness is pressed right between my legs. I look up and see the storm in his eyes. Oh god.

What have I gotten myself into?

———

Brad

When she presses her petal-soft lips against me, I lose it. Every shred of decency I have in me is gone right out the window. It's fucking *gone*.

Her lips are a button shooting straight to my cock. It swells to its full girth, pressing against the zipper of my jeans.

And my god, the way she tastes…like milk and honey.

Hallelujah. I've found the promised land.

Her sweet, little virginal pussy is pressed right up

against my cock, and I want to rub against her and dry hump her like a lovesick schoolboy.

Her eyes are wide again like maybe she's doubting offering herself to me, and I have to take deep breaths to get myself under control.

I should set her down, but I don't. God help me, but I can't. Not yet.

I walk back over to the leather-covered seat and sit with her still held up against me, her legs straddling me.

"Do you want to do this, Poppy?" I ask her.

She looks at me, her eyes lined by thick lashes. "It's what you paid for, isn't it?" she asks tentatively.

I shake my head. "I didn't pay for this."

The color seems to drain from her face, and her hands drop from around my neck. I instantly mourn the loss of them as she says, "Oh my god, this is so embarrassing. You don't want me."

She makes a move to get up, but I hold her in place, unwilling to let her go just yet. "Sweetheart," I let out a ragged breath, "do I *feel* like a man who doesn't want you?"

Her eyes widen again and then she blushes as she realizes what I'm talking about. "But you said you didn't..."

I cut her off by explaining, "Some of my old

college buddies apparently set this up without my knowledge. I'm not in the habit of buying women. Christ, it's not that I don't want you, Poppy. I don't think I've ever wanted someone more in my entire fucking life, but you deserve better than this. I don't want you to do something you don't want to do."

Her eyes seem to soften at my words. Then, she takes a deep breath and says bravely, "I—I think I could do this…you know…with you." She looks down and then peeks up at me with pink cheeks.

I groan, unable to resist pulling her lips to mine again with her looking at me like that. When I push my tongue into her mouth, she melts against me, and I can't stop the rush of male pride that fills me.

I cup her ass with one hand while I slide the other one between us to feel her through her panties, all the while never breaking from kissing her.

I hiss in a breath. She's fucking soaked. She wants this too—at least her body does—and that knowledge alone is almost enough to make me come in my pants right now.

I want nothing more than to pull her panties to the side and plunge right into her, but she's a virgin, and I know she needs to be prepared for her first time.

I pull back from her lips long enough to lift her

dress up over her head. Her hands automatically go to cover her breasts, but I gently pull them away from her. "Don't hide from me, pretty baby," I tell her, as my eyes rove over her milky orbs with their dusky peaks, trailing down over a lithe stomach and settling on her lacy white panties that are sitting right on my crotch.

"Jesus, you're fucking beautiful," I tell her reverently, and she blushes before I lean in and lick one of her hard nipples.

She gasps and shakes at the contact, and I smile against her skin as I continue to flick my tongue on her hard nub.

"Oh," she moans as her arms go back around my head. I latch onto the nipple and suck, and she begins to move against me, seeking friction.

My cock surges even more at the sensation of her dragging her cunt up and down it, but I can't tolerate it for very long before I still her with a hand on her hip.

I flip her over, laying her down on the leather bench, hovering atop her, my arms on either side of her. Her hair splays out around her head, and her lips are red and swollen from my kisses.

I've never seen anything so fucking beautiful in all my life. I want to devour her. Every inch of her. But I know that once I get a taste of her, I won't be able to stop. That's why I ask her, "Are you sure want to do this, baby?"

She opens her mouth to answer, but before she can speak, I add, "I mean, do you *want* to do this? You're not just doing it for the money because I swear if you don't want this, you can tell me to stop right now and I will, and you'll still get paid. I'll make sure of it."

She hesitates for a moment, considering, and I'm halfway expecting her to change her mind. She told me she was doing this for the money, and while it might fucking kill me, I meant what I told her. I'll stop if she tells me.

Somehow I'll stop.

***

Poppy

He's put me on the spot.

He's not going to let me pretend that I'm only doing this for the money. He's promised me I'll get it either way.

He wants me to *want* to do this with him.

If I had any sense of self-preservation, I'd take

him up on his offer. I'd take the money and keep my virginity intact.

But as I look up at his hardened jaw and see the slight tremble in the taut muscles of his arms, I can see that this incredibly hot man really does want me. It's like he's barely holding himself back. And that knowledge does something to me.

It makes me feel sexy and desired—not to mention the response my body has to him. There's a strange ache between my legs that caused me to rub against his hard length when he was kissing my breasts. The delicious friction helped ease the ache, but it's still there.

Somehow I know that Brad knows how to take it away. That he'll show me where that aching leads to if I'll just let him.

I don't know anything about this man, other than he's the hottest man I've ever laid eyes on.

Is it wrong of me to want to give myself to this stranger I've known all of ten minutes? Like Melissa said, most girls have a horrible first time with boys they know. Something tells me even though I don't know Brad, he'll make sure my first time is worth remembering.

He's still holding himself up above me, his eyes burning down into mine, waiting for my answer.

This is crazy, but it's a hell of a lot better than what I was prepared to do. *So much better*. I'd been prepared to give it up to some dirty old man.

I take a deep breath before nodding and telling him, "Yes, I want this."

He exhales a harsh breath before saying, "Thank fuck," his lips crashing down to mine again.

He steals my breath away, kissing me with a passion I've only ever read about in romance novels, his tongue swirling with mine before he slows the kiss, nipping and licking gently at my lips.

His kisses move down my jaw, over the column of my throat, over my breasts and then over my stomach, branding everywhere he touches with wet heat.

He keeps kissing his way down, down until his head is hovering above my most intimate of places. He kisses the insides of my thighs, the sensation of his lips on them causing them to tremble. That place between my legs is burning, aching, needing something, and I can't stop the whimper that escapes me.

"Please," I beg him, not knowing quite what I'm begging for but knowing that I need something.

Then, he looks up at me and without ever breaking eye contact, he licks me *there*, running his tongue all along my slit and dragging it up. The look in his eyes is dark and hungry. It makes my heart beat wildly.

My head falls back on the bench as a strangled gasp escapes me, sparks going off between my legs. Never, ever, ever, could I have imagined it would feel like *that* to have a man kiss me there.

He follows his lick with an open-mouth kiss, and then he begins flicking his tongue back and forth over this spot that sends tremors up and down my spine. I try to close my legs, the sensation too much, but he holds them open, his tongue steadily licking that spot over and over again.

He moans against my flesh while he licks, and then I feel one of his fingers enter me.

I instantly stiffen at the foreign invasion, but he soothes me with, "Relax, sweetheart." He barely lifts his mouth off me, and I feel the words fan against my skin before he's licking and sucking on that spot again, his finger slowly moving in and out of me.

The exquisite pressure mixed with his licks have my nerve endings buzzing and snapping. I feel another finger enter me, and I feel impossibly full as he continues to lick that little nub of pleasure and stroke his fingers slowly in and out of me.

"Please," I'm babbling incoherently, "I can't..."

He finally latches onto that nub and increases his

suction on it as his fingers move in and out of me faster now, that incredible pressure building and building until it bursts into blinding light.

I shatter, a sob breaking forth from my lips as my entire body shakes.

"Fuck yes," he growls as he continues to lick between my shaking legs.

I look down at him, the sight of his big shoulders between my legs the most erotic thing I've ever seen.

Then, his head comes up and his eyes meet mine again as he stalks his way up the length of my body.

I'm having trouble breathing as his intense blue eyes gaze down at me with burning heat.

"So fucking beautiful," he says before his lips meet mine.

I taste myself on him as he kisses me deeply while unzipping himself. He pulls back from me long enough to shed his shirt and pull down his pants, and my eyes widen at all the male glory revealed to me.

His muscles bunch and ripple with every movement, and my eyes travel down a hard chest and sculpted abs to that hard part of him jutting out from between his legs.

I gulp. It's thick and long and veiny, and I don't see any way it can possibly fit inside me. The tip of it glistens with moisture, and he strokes it a couple of times root to tip as he looks down at me.

He groans before spreading my legs and positioning himself between them. "This might hurt at first, sweetheart," he tells me. "If you need me to slow down, just tell me, okay?"

I swallow and nod, and then I feel a growing pressure as he pushes slowly into me. My fingers go up to grip his arms tightly. It feels like he's rending me in two and he's barely gotten the tip in.

I whimper, and he leans down over me, placing his elbows on either side of my head and angling my head up to kiss me.

His tongue languidly stroking mine distracts me. I tremble at his kiss. Although I can still feel the pressure between my legs, his kiss is causing a low thrumming sensation to pound throughout my skin.

He stops kissing me for a moment as he groans deeply, his arms shaking. He stops pressing into me and looks into my eyes again, asking me, "Are you okay, beautiful?"

"Yes," my voice comes out breathy. "That wasn't so bad," I smile up at him.

He gives a dry chuckle. "I'm not even halfway there, baby."

My eyes widen. There's more? He groans again

before his lips crash back to mine, kissing me more urgently this time. He moves them to the side of my throat where he continues kissing and sucking before he moves down to my nipple, sending currents of pleasure throughout me. He's still not moving, but then he suddenly thrusts deep with his hips, tearing through me.

He muffles the sound of my cry by pressing my head against the crook of his neck. My arms wrap around him, my nails clawing at his back as I cling to him.

"I'm sorry, sweetheart," he whispers against my hair before dropping a kiss there. I'm still gasping, but the pain eventually starts to subside as he drops kisses all over my face whispering how beautiful I am. I almost can't believe it. This gorgeous man thinks I'm beautiful. He desires me.

"Does it still hurt?" he asks me, genuine concern in his voice.

I shake my head. "Not as much, but there's this pressure." My brow furrows as I try to shift my hips to get more comfortable.

His breath hitches and he curses as my movement causes him to move slightly within me. I let out a gasp of my own when the movement causes him to hit this spot inside me that sends tingles deep within me.

Never taking his eyes off me, he pulls back slightly before pushing back in, hitting that spot again. I moan, and his eyes heat. "You like that, sweetheart?"

"Yes," I don't hesitate to tell him, lifting my hips up a bit to try to recapture the sensation.

"Holy fuck," he says. "You're perfect."

Then, he begins pulling more of his length out of me before stroking it back in. The friction is building something inside me into an inferno, and I wrap my legs around his waist, lifting my hips up to meet his thrusts, desperate to feel that delicious tingle deep inside me every time he hits that spot.

He groans raggedly when my legs wrap around him, his thrusts picking up pace. He clutches me tight to his chest, slamming in and out of me now. I've never felt so full in my life, and I can't think. All I can do is feel him pounding into me over and over again, the pressure and tingles building and building.

"Not gonna fucking last, baby," he growls in my ear as he keeps pounding. It's impossible, but I feel the length of him growing even harder as he continues to push into me, and then he hits that spot hard one more time, and I explode.

I cry out, clinging to him, every muscle in my body contracting before I go lax, coming down from a wave of pleasure so intense it takes my breath away.

"Jesus," he croaks before he moans, grabbing my hips with both his hands and thrusting deep into me one last time. I feel hot liquid shooting deep within me, coating my insides.

His deep moans are the sexiest thing I've ever heard. He continues to pump into me, spraying his spend into me until it overflows onto my thighs and drips down my butt.

His breathing is heavy as he holds himself inside me, stroking the sides of my face, looking down at me like I'm the most precious thing on the planet.

My heart is melting at the look in his eyes, and I can't help wishing he'd hold me like this forever.

Chapter Three

Brad

Mine. Fucking *mine.*

That's all I can think as I stare down at this beautiful little angel laying underneath me.

I was the first one to claim her, and fuck me, if all I can think about is being the last.

The way she trustingly gave herself to me. The way she fell apart underneath me. Christ, this girl was the perfect virgin, fucking me back eagerly, stroke for stroke, her face the picture of sinful innocence the entire time.

I want to give her the fucking world. I want to know everything about her.

I never want to let her go.

But she's staring up at me with those beautiful doe-brown eyes, and I know I can't lay inside her forever—no matter how much I may want to.

So, I sit up, pulling out of her, grabbing some napkins off the table and dipping them into my water glass before gently wiping the blood and cum from her. I feel a moment of remorse as I do so. This princess deserved so much more than to lose her virginity this way.

I don't wipe her off of me, instead just pulling my pants up and tucking myself away still coated in her juices. I help her sit up and then slip her white dress back over her before stroking her hair over her shoulders and gently kissing her lips.

She still doesn't speak as she watches me put my shirt on.

"Poppy, I—" I begin, but I never get to finish telling her that I don't want this to be a one-time thing, that I want to take her home with me and spoil her rotten and never let her go, because at that inopportune moment Eric bursts back into the room with two girls hanging off him.

"Oh, hey, man. I didn't know you were still here.

Figured you were long gone by now," he says, palming one girl's tits and another one's ass.

I scowl at him, getting ready to tell him to get the fuck out, but then the room floods with more girls he's apparently invited in for a private party just for him. They're all giggling and obviously drunk, and he's grinning like the stupid idiot he is.

I turn back to grab Poppy and go somewhere more private where we can talk, but she's gone, having slipped off the second my back was turned.

I feel a dark pit churning in my stomach at the thought of never seeing her again and jump up, rushing out of the door to the private room to look for her. I check the front and back exits, but there's no sign of her anywhere.

The most perfect girl I've ever met is gone. I don't have her last name or phone number or any way to get in contact with her again.

I stomp back into the private room and grab Eric up by the collar.

"What the fuck, man?" he says.

"Where'd you find her?" I demand.

"Who?" he asks before comprehension dawns and a sly grin takes over. "Oh, the escort." He laughs, "You ready for round two already? I take it was she was good."

I think about rearing back and pummeling him for talking about her that way, but then he laughs and answers, telling me the name of the escort service.

I release him, and he stumbles back, still laughing before calling out behind me as I walk away, "Yeah, you're welcome, man! And happy birthday again!"

———

Poppy

Tears are streaming down my cheeks. I know it's nonsensical for me to feel this way. I shouldn't feel hurt that Brad's friend showed up with a slew of girls with him for the two of them.

Brad is gorgeous, so it shouldn't surprise me he's a playboy. But…but the way he'd held me so tenderly as if I was the most precious thing in the world…I wanted it to last forever.

Which is completely ridiculous since I don't know him at all. He's just some stranger whose friends had paid for him to have sex with me. I was a birthday gift to slack his lust—nothing more.

He probably thinks I'm nothing but a common whore since I had sex with him for money. I frown. But he offered to make sure I got paid anyway even if

I didn't have sex with him. That doesn't quite fit with the picture I'm painting of him in my mind, but whatever. What does it matter now?

He gave me the best first time a girl could hope for, and now it's over. I saved us both the embarrassment of an awkward goodbye by seizing my opportunity and slipping from the room the moment it filled with scantily clad women.

But I wish…I wish we'd met under different circumstances. I wish there was a way we could be something more.

I've never been into guys much. Never even dated. Just like making lasting friendships, it had been too difficult to develop any kind of relationship with a guy when I'd been shuffled through the system so much.

I mean, I've crushed on a few movie stars like any normal teenage girl, but I've never seen a *real* man who could make my knees go weak with longing.

Brad is like a Greek god, devastatingly handsome and carved from stone. My tummy fills with butterflies just thinking of how small I felt in his big arms, how he'd looked at me.

Crazily enough, I felt safe with him, trusting him completely with my virginity. He showed me more pleasure than I ever knew was possible.

But what if he's doing that same thing right now with those other girls? My heart breaks at the thought before I sit up straight on my little cot and resolutely dry my eyes.

This is ridiculous. I have no claim on him. I was just an escort hired to please him. That's all. I'm probably just overly emotional since it was my first time. Haven't I read in books about how a lot of girls cry after their first time? Surely that's all this is.

It's all it would have to be. He's long gone, and I need to just be thankful he gave me a gentler first time than I'd been prepared for.

It's time to look to my future. That's why I did this anyway, for a chance to begin a new life.

I just hadn't counted on that new life being haunted by dreams of Brad's kisses and touches on my skin.

Brad

Of course, the madam of the high-dollar escort service wouldn't tell me shit. No manner of bribing or coaxing would get the impenetrable woman to budge. She protected her clients' and workers' confidentiality.

Part of me is relieved that Poppy went through an agency that runs such a tight ship. I don't have to worry about some obsessive fuck—like me—finding out her personal information.

But dammit, I'm at a dead end, and I feel like I'm going insane.

Why the fuck didn't I get her last name?

I was intending to. I wanted to learn everything I could about her. If Eric hadn't busted in when he did with a whole harem of girls, I'd have convinced her to come back to my place with me where we'd have talked about everything and I'd have begged her to let me keep her forever.

As it is, here I am two weeks later, no closer to finding her than I was that first night she slipped away from me. It's not for lack of trying either. I've searched every "Poppy" I can find on social media. Apparently, she doesn't have a social media account, or if she does, I haven't found it.

I've walked the streets aimlessly, doing a double-take every time I saw a tiny silhouette with long dark hair just to make sure it isn't her.

But I know. I always know it isn't her. I think I'd recognize her instantly from any angle if I ever saw her again. Hell, I think my soul would recognize her presence before my eyes ever did.

I've become broody, sitting for hours at my desk in my home office, staring out at nothing, reliving every touch of her skin. That night is permanently branded into my brain, and all I can do is replay those moments in my head over and over again until I finally have to yank down my pants and relieve myself with my fist, pretending it's her tight, virginal pussy.

Remembering the look of shocked ecstasy on her face the first time she came when I was eating her sweet pussy does me in every time. I can still see her brown eyes staring up at me innocently, trustingly, and it fells me every time.

I have this insane need to protect her, and it's killing me that I don't know where she is or if she's okay.

I curse and try my best to push the thoughts of her out of my mind. It's no fucking good, but I have to try anyway. My first class of the semester starts in just a few minutes, and it won't be fair to my students to not give them my undivided attention.

I've already got the syllabi printed out and laying in a pile on my desk. I usually enjoy my job and look forward to the first day of classes when I can meet all the new potential. It's always interesting to learn which medium each art student is most attracted to. Of course, they'll learn about a bit of all of them in my class, but all artists have a preference. Mine is sculpting, but I haven't had my hands in clay since my birthday. All I want to feel under my fingertips is the softness of her skin. All I want to mold is her skin to my body, tracing my hands and tongue along each curve.

I pass a hand over my face and sigh. *Fuck me.*

I glance down at my watch just as the first of the new students begin to filter into the room. I'd normally greet them warmly, seeking to set them at ease. But I just don't have it in me today. I'll wait until they're all here and get through this as best I can.

As the last of the students file in and take a seat, I glance down at my watch again. When I see it's time for class to begin, I step up from my desk and move to stand behind my podium, beginning my welcome spill.

I've just finished introducing myself and have begun launching into what students can expect in my class when I hear the door open to the side of me.

I give a loud sigh. While I try not to be a total hardass, one thing I can't stand is tardiness. Students coming in late shows a lack of respect and interrupts everything.

"You're," I begin as I turn to the door, ready to say 'late,' but the word dies on my lips before I can ever voice it.

It's *her*.

I blink my eyes, half thinking I've finally lost it and am seeing things, but she's still there when I reopen them.

Those brown locks are pulled up into a ponytail, a few strands falling out to frame her angelic face. Her puffy pink lips are as sinfully innocent as I remember, but this time instead of wearing a virginal white dress, she's wearing leggings and an oversized sweater that's falling off one shoulder. She's adorably disheveled like she knows she's running late, and my god, I want to devour her.

Jesus. I'm glad I'm standing behind the podium. Otherwise, the entire classroom would be treated to the sight of what her presence does to me. My cock is making an obscene tent in my pants, and I grip the sides of the podium so tight I'm surprised the wood doesn't splinter beneath my grip. It takes everything in me not to run over and grab her. Sling her over my shoulder like a caveman and take her back to my lair. Lock her up where I'll never lose her again.

Her soft brown eyes are big as she looks at me and the recognition passes over her face.

Her face flushes prettily, and all that sight does is make me remember how that flush traveled down to her breasts when her little body was underneath me.

I realize I'm still staring at her, so I clear my throat and say, "Please have a seat, Miss—?" I raise an eyebrow at her questioningly. I'm damn sure not going to miss the opportunity to get her last name now.

Hell, I know I'd have noticed any students with her first name on my roster. She must have been added into my class at the last minute and the Registar hasn't given me the updated class list.

"Montgomery," she answers as she rushes to an open seat at the back of the classroom—as far away from me as she can possibly get.

"Miss Montgomery," I repeat as I incline my head toward her before continuing on.

I'm droning on with the basic welcome speech. I don't know how I'm focusing on what I'm saying. I guess I've been doing this for so long I could do it in my sleep. My blood is rushing in my veins, and my eyes keep drifting back to her.

I've been searching for her for weeks, and now she waltzes right into my classroom. My heart is beating a staccato rhythm in tune with my thoughts. My student. She's my student.

The universe is a cruel bitch.

———

Poppy

Oh my god. *Oh my god.*

It's *him.*

Brad is my art professor.

My art professor.

Holy shit.

I feel like his eyes are searing me every time they land on me.

Could this get any more awkward?

Brad—I mean, Professor Davenport—I can't think of him as Brad anymore, can I? He's my professor now.

Is it unbearably hot in here, or am I just on fire from my flaming cheeks?

How am I ever going to be able to look him in the eyes?

I'm looking down at the desk now, anywhere but at him, but I feel his gaze every time it lands on me. His eyes are scorching me with their heat.

He's seen me naked. He's…he's done things to me. Delicious, sinful things. Things that I still dream about every night. I can't count how many times I've woken up in the middle of the night these past two weeks, drenched and aching after dreaming of that one time.

I've tried touching myself the way he did, but I can never replicate that feeling he gave me. I can never bring myself to climax the way he did.

That night was the highlight of my pathetic life, and as much as I've tried to forget him, I can't.

And now in some ironic twist of fate I'm his student.

I can't do this. I'm going to have to drop this class. There's no way I can sit here in this burning humiliation every day.

I don't hear a word he's saying, but he's suddenly passing out the class syllabus, prowling among the desks like a lion.

An insanely gorgeous, sexy lion.

And the way his eyes keep burning into mine leaves no question as to who his prey is.

He reaches me last since I'm at the back of the classroom. "A word with you after class, Miss Montgomery?" he asks me softly as he places the syllabus in my shaking hands.

I swallow and nod resignedly, not trusting myself to speak.

He makes his way back to the front of the classroom, talks for a couple more minutes, and then dismisses everyone.

Everyone but me that is.

I take my time putting my syllabus away in my pink backpack, trying to make myself as inconspicuous as possible.

When the last student finally files out of the room, Brad motions for me to follow him into his office.

My heart is keeping tune with my steps, each one like a drum leading me to my execution.

He stands back and holds the door open for me, making me have to pass before him to get inside. I feel the heat emanating off his body as I do so, and my breath catches.

He slams the door shut behind us, and I jump, looking up at him as he towers over me.

"Poppy," he breaths.

"Professor Davenport, I had no idea. I swear. If I'd have known—"

He cuts me off with a frown as he corrects me, "Brad. I'm Brad, remember?"

My breath hitches as I whisper, "Yes, I remember."

His hands ball into fists at his sides, and I take a step back, thinking he's angry.

And he is.

"Why did you slip off like that?" he bites out.

"What?" My brow furrows.

"That night…you left before we had a chance to talk." He seems deeply disturbed that I left with no word.

"What was there to say?" I ask him. "You got what you paid for and your party obviously wasn't over. I didn't want to be in your way." I hope he can't hear the hurt in my voice at the thought of him doing to those other women what he did to me.

His frown only deepens. "There was plenty to say, and that wasn't my party. That was my stupid college buddy being the dickhead that he is."

I just look at him. Is he saying he didn't stick around and have sex with those women?

Comprehension seems to dawn on him, and he curses, "I'll fucking kill Eric," before he takes a step toward me. "I tried to find you as soon as you were gone, Poppy. I've been looking for you for two weeks." He shakes his head and a hollow laugh escapes him.

My heart soars in hope. He's been looking for me? He wanted to see me again?

"And now here you are dropped right into my

classroom. A student. A *fucking* student." He runs a hand over his face, and my heart plummets.

Of course, we can't be anything more. I'm his student. It's unethical on every level. He could lose his job.

And I don't want to be known as the girl who dates her professor. I don't want my achievements clouded by any sort of scandal. I certainly don't want people to question how I earned my grades.

"I get it," I tell him, my heart in my throat. "I'll talk to my advisor. See if I can be moved to another class."

"Like hell you will," he snaps.

I blink. "Excuse me?"

"The only other art professor on this campus who teaches this class is Chapman, and I'll be damned if I'll have that motherfucker ogling you."

I raise my chin defiantly. He may have taken my virginity, and he might be hot as hell, but he's not going to tell me what to do. "Well, that's not your decision. I just think it would be easier if—"

He cuts me off again with a harsh laugh. "Nothing is going to make this easier, sweetheart."

My pulse quickens at the way he calls me sweetheart. It reminds me of how he whispered it in my ear that night as he held me close.

I know he's thinking the same thing because he begins to walk slowly toward me. For each step he takes forward, I take a step back until my back hits the front of his desk and I have nowhere else to go.

He stops, leaving mere inches between us, and I'm having difficulty breathing with him this much in my space. My thoughts are scrambled and I can hardly think.

He reaches out and runs a finger along my bare shoulder, trailing it up my neck, leaving goosebumps in his wake. His face looms closer to mine, and I know he means to kiss me.

As much as I want him to, I force myself to place my hands on his chest and push him back.

His eyes heat at my touch, his gazing flicking down to where my hands rest on his chest.

I can't let this happen. If he kisses me, it will likely lead to more, and I can't have him thinking he can use me for a quick fuck anytime he feels like it just because his friends once paid for me. I have more self-respect than that.

Guilt pricks my conscience as I realize that he doesn't know that, though. He doesn't know the kind of girl I really am. I sold myself to him. He doesn't know that was the hardest decision of my life. He probably thinks I'm just a slut with no self-respect.

And maybe that's right because what self-respecting girl would sell her virginity the way I did?

I take advantage of the extra inches I've put between us and slip from between him and the desk, making a beeline for the door. "I have to go, Professor Davenport," I say.

"Poppy, wait!" he calls out behind me, but I'm already rushing out of the door, determined to put distance between us.

It's better this way. I can't allow us to repeat what happened that night. There's no way we can carry on a public relationship, and I'm not going to be a secret.

Professor Davenport and I can't happen.

Chapter Four

Brad

I watch Poppy flee from me like I'm the devil himself. Damn it all to hell. Maybe I am. What kind of guy takes a girl's virginity in the private room of a bar? A girl he doesn't know, one his idiotic college buddies paid for.

No wonder she keeps running from me.

It was everything I could do to keep my hands off her when I had her in my office. I was *this* close to kissing her. *This* close to pushing her up on my desk and fucking her with all the pent-up worry and frustration I've felt looking for her for the past two weeks.

Fuck, what am I going to do? She's my student, so she's off limits if I want to keep my job. I don't think

I'll be able to sneak around with her. Not only for the fact that I don't think there's any way I could keep my obsession with her a secret if she lets me have her again but also for the simple fact that she seems to want nothing to do with me.

My cock is still rock hard, and I can still smell the flowery scent of her in the room. I pull my aching rod from my slacks and begin to stroke it.

It's probably insane of me to be jacking off to a girl who literally just bolted from me, but I don't give a fuck. All it takes is five pumps of me picturing her standing here, her hair in a ponytail, her puffy pink lips, and I'm splashing cum onto the tile floor, wishing I was coming inside her sweet pussy instead.

When I'm done, I slump against the desk, my arms aching to hold her.

It's more than just sex I want from her. I want all of her. Every bit of her. Every breath. Every sigh. Every thought. I want *her*. I want her so bad it hurts.

But it looks like I can't have the one thing I want more than life itself.

But that won't stop me from learning everything I can about her. That won't stop me from making sure she's safe.

———

Poppy

I can't drop Brad's class without falling below a full-time student status. The other art class is filled up. Hell, almost everything suitable for freshmen is filled up. I was lucky to get the classes I did registering so late in the game.

So here I am again sitting at the back of his classroom as far away from him as I can get.

It doesn't work, though. I can still feel the heat of his eyes as they land on me triumphantly. Like he knew I wouldn't be able to drop his class.

"So before we jump into everything, let's learn a bit more about each other. When I call your name, please tell everyone what your favorite art form is and why. I'll start."

He looks right into my eyes as he says, "Mine's sculpting. I like to shape things with my hands, feel the form mold and give way underneath them."

I feel like there's a hidden message in his words, like he's referring to that night, and my knees tremble under the table as I break away from his gaze, looking down at the desk.

A few girls in the front of the classroom giggle, but he ignores them. Of course, he has female students who have crushes on him. He's gorgeous. I try to ignore the sting of jealousy that creeps up within me.

He's apparently going down the rows, calling on each student starting in the front of the classroom and working his way back, saving me for last.

I also can't stop thinking about how it's fitting that he likes sculpting. He's more sculpted than any sculpture I've ever seen, though. I remember the way he ran his hands over my body that night, as if he was molding *me*.

I shake my head and make myself focus.

One of the girls in the front says she likes glasswork. A guy in the middle likes metalwork. Another girl likes photography.

When Brad reaches me, I answer without hesitation, "Painting, most specifically impressionist-style paintings. I like the way I can paint an impression of something the way I see it. It's like I can create a better view of the world."

The guy sitting next to me grins at me and commends me, "Great answer, beautiful."

Is it just my imagination, or does Brad seem to stiffen from where he stands behind the podium? His eyes rake over the guy as if silently berating him for speaking during his class before he moves on to his lecture about art history.

I take notes like everyone else, but there really is no need. I know I'll remember everything he said.

He's riveting. I can hear the passion in his voice when he talks about art. It's the same passion I have, and he really is a good teacher. He presents everything in a way that's easy to understand as he clicks through the slides, drawing our attention to different details in the paintings, sculptures, and other art forms he shows us.

All too soon class is over, and I hasten to put my things in my bag so I can rush to the door. I don't want to get caught alone with him again.

I might have to be in his class, but I don't have to put myself through any unnecessary torture.

"Hey, beautiful. Poppy, right?" the guy who's been sitting next to me all class period asks.

"Yeah," I barely glance up at him in my haste to get my things and leave.

"I'm Jason." His name barely registers with me. I'm so focused on jetting out of here. "You wanna grab a bite sometime?"

I look up at him then. He's not unattractive, but he's certainly no Brad. I try to give him an apologetic smile as I decline, "No, thanks."

I feel Brad's eyes burning a hole into me from the front of the classroom, but I refuse to look at him.

The guy shrugs. "If you ever change your mind…"

I nod at him before excusing myself and practically sprinting for the door.

———

Brad

She's avoiding me. She arrives barely on time, making sure there are no minutes to spare. No extra moments where I might steal a few seconds with her. Every day after class she's one of the first ones to hit the door. She sits in the very back of the classroom and avoids my eyes like I've got the goddamned plague or something.

My jaw clenches when I remember that prick asking her out on the first day of class. Thank God she said no. Still, I had to stop myself from doing something petty like docking the jackass' grade for no reason just for daring to breathe in her direction.

I'm well aware my obsession with her goes beyond the norm.

Not only is she gorgeous, but she's the perfect student. Her eyes are bright and interested during class. She's intelligent and enjoys the subject matter. She's aced every impromptu quiz I've given.

I allow her the distance she puts between us. If it makes her more comfortable, I won't press her. Maybe it's for the best—no matter how much I want to drag her home with me and never let her go.

That wouldn't be fair to her. She's here to get a college education like everyone else. I can't deprive her of that opportunity.

I can't help wondering if this is what she needed the money for, if this is why she sold her beautiful body to a stranger.

I suspect it is. In finding out everything I could about her, I found out about how her parents died when she was a little girl, how she'd been passed from foster home to foster home, about the shitty diner she worked in in exchange for a room to rent in the back of the place.

God, how I wish I'd have known. If I'd have known, I'd have rescued her from all that.

But she's stronger than she looks and determined. Her drive reminds me of my own. She made a terrible sacrifice and did what she had to do to try to make a better life for herself.

I watch her go into the building where I know she shares a dorm with her friend. My daily routine. After my classes, I sit in my office until her last class ends, and then I follow her, silently watching to make sure she gets back to her dorm okay.

Contrary to what a lot of people think, college campuses aren't the safest places in the world. Too many raging hormones and horny motherfuckers out there who wouldn't think twice about raping a beautiful young coed.

I just want to make sure Poppy is safe. That's what I tell myself anyway. Hell, the way I'm stalking her, she more likely needs protection from me.

But I'd never hurt her.

You already have hurt her, a voice in the back of my mind says. *You let her sell you her virginity, and you're not even sorry. You'd do it all over again.*

No, I'm not sorry I took her virginity. I am sorry about *how* it all came about. I wish I had met her another way. I wish I'd given her the romantic first time she deserved.

I wish she was mine, dammit. In my mind, she is. I claimed her. More than our bodies joined that night. Our souls became one too. She's my other half, and I don't know how long I can go on like this, letting her steer clear of me and pretend we never happened.

I don't allow myself to think about if she's been

with another guy since that night. I want to slam my fist through the wall every time the thought creeps into my head.

Something tells me she hasn't, and I have to believe that. Otherwise, I'll go mad with jealousy.

It's hard enough not to beat down every mother-fucker who looks her way. I see the appreciative glances she gets from all these young pricks. More than one has tried to talk to her, but she's made it clear she's not interested—thank fuck.

Of course, that doesn't mean she wants shit to do with me either. And maybe I'm a selfish asshole, but if she's not with me, I don't want her with anyone else.

I know that my behavior is irrational. I know that if the board knew I was obsessively stalking a student, my ass would be booted out the door so fast. God help me, but I can't find it in myself to care anymore. All I care about is knowing where she is at all times, knowing that no one else touches her.

At least if she stays single, I can stay her silent protector. I can watch over her without her knowing.

It's better than nothing. And at this point, I'll take whatever I can get.

———

Poppy

"I can't believe I let you talk me into this," I grumble to Melissa as we walk to the frat house, our heels clicking on the pavement.

"Oh, lighten up, Poppy. You can't be all work and no play. All you do is study. You never come out with me. We're in college! We're supposed to party a little bit."

I glance over at Melissa who looks like a typical party girl in her skintight nude dress that clings to every curve of her body and leaves nothing to the imagination.

She forbade me to wear my normal outfit of leggings and a sweater. Instead, she dolled me up in one of her short black skirts and a silky gold top. She blew my hair out, and it hangs down my back in soft waves. I'm wearing a pair of dangly gold earrings she insisted I wear along with sky-high heels I can barely walk in.

It's obvious where Melissa's been spending her money.

"I look ridiculous," I mutter.

"You look amazing!" she counters, glancing over at me with a frown. "What you need is some alcohol. It'll help you unwind."

Now it's my turn to frown at her. "We're not even old enough to drink, Melissa. It's illegal."

She shrugs like it's no big deal. "So are some other things we've done, but that didn't stop us then."

I close my mouth, her point taken. Selling our virginity wasn't exactly legal either, was it?

Honestly, I don't know why I let Melissa talk me into this party. I'm not the party girl type. I'm the stay-in-her-dorm-and-fantasize-over-what-can-never-be-with-her-professor type. I grimace at the thought.

Of course, I haven't told Melissa anything about Brad. I haven't talked to her about that night at all. I want to keep him all to myself. She hasn't said much about her night either except that she got through it and wanted to forget all about it.

Whatever happened with Melissa and whoever she got paired up with doesn't seem to have fazed her too much. She's like my same old best friend, only richer.

And I'm my same old boring self except that I feel like I can never be the same again.

I can never forget him.

Especially since he's my art professor.

I grimace again.

"You know what? Maybe you're right," I tell her.

She grins at me as we walk up the steps to the brick frat house. "That's the spirit, girl!"

Music is bumping and lights are flashing as we enter the house. We're immediately greeted by a couple of guys. "Hey, ladies! Looking good!"

Melissa seems to know one of them. He's probably the one who invited her. They greet one another with a hug, and then she takes off with him, leaving me by myself.

I'm feeling completely abandoned and more than a little pissed. Why was it so important for me to come to this thing with her if she was going to immediately ditch me? Not like I expected her to stick by me all night, but seriously? As soon as we walk through the door?

I stand here awkwardly. The other dude—a muscular guy with sandy blond hair—is still standing in front of me checking me out. When my eyes meet his, he smiles at me and asks, "Do you want a drink?"

"Sure," I tell him, almost having to scream to be heard over the music blaring over the speakers. Maybe a drink will relax me enough where I can become more comfortable. I feel so out of place.

He's gone for only a moment. When he returns, he hands me a red solo cup, and I take a tentative sip.

It's some kind of punch spiked with something, but at least it doesn't taste horrible.

"I'm Nick," he tells me. "What's your name?"

"Poppy," I answer back, looking up at him. He's taller than me, of course, but almost everyone is, though I don't think he's as tall as Brad. I stop my thoughts right there. I can't keeping comparing every guy I meet to Brad.

"You wanna dance, pretty Poppy?" he asks me with a smile that would probably make plenty of other girls' hearts melt.

I don't really want to, but I know it's ridiculous to come to a party and just stand there, so I let him lead me to the dance floor.

I take a few more sips of my drink for courage and then start swaying to the beat of the music. Nick is dancing behind me, and I don't know if it's the alcohol or what, but I feel myself starting to relax.

"You've got moves, babe," Nick leans down to tell me.

I take another sip of my drink before telling him, "So do you."

He grins at me. He's really an attractive-looking guy. Too bad I'm still dreaming about Brad every night. Has he ruined me for any other man?

I shake those thoughts off and dance some more.

Nick's hands eventually move to my hips, and he pulls me closer. Too close.

I pull away and shout at him over the music, "I'm just gonna get some air," before I head for the doorway.

The booze is catching up with me. Things aren't exactly spinning, but I'm definitely feeling the effects of whatever was in that punch. I need to slow down.

I step out into the crisp night and take a deep breath. I should probably just go back to the dorm. Melissa ditched me, and I haven't seen her since. I doubt I'll be missed.

"Leaving so soon?" Nick asks me as I start to step down from the huge stone porch. I didn't realize he'd followed me outside.

"Yeah," I answer sheepishly. "This isn't really my scene. I came for my friend more than anything. And she pretty much ditched me as soon as we got here," I give a dry laugh before continuing, "so I think I'm just going to go ahead and call it a night."

"Well, that sucks," he says, "but at least let me walk you back to your dorm. You do live on campus, don't you?"

"Yeah," I nod, "but you really don't have to do that. I don't want to take you away from your party."

He shrugs. "It's no big deal. There'll be a million more just like them."

"Well, thanks then," I smile at him, and we start walking in the direction of my building.

"So what's your major?" he asks me, making small talk.

"Art," I tell him.

He raises an eyebrow, and I shrug. "Yeah, I know. It's considered a frivolous major, but it's what I love."

He laughs.

"What's yours?" I ask him, being polite more than anything else. It's not that I totally don't care, but I it's not like I'm dying to know more about him either. Nick seems like a nice enough guy. I'm just not interested and can't wait to get back to my dorm room.

"Economics," he answers.

"Wow," I say as I start to sway, struggling to maintain my balance. My limbs feel heavy, and I'm starting to feel like I can't walk straight.

"You okay?" he asks me, but I notice that he doesn't sound really surprised by my suddenly woozy state, and that instantly puts me on alert.

I tell myself I'm just being paranoid as I answer him, "Yeah, just—" I stumble and he catches me by wrapping his hands around my waist.

He chuckles, and then he starts to pull me in another direction from where my dorm room is.

"Wait, my dorm…it's that way," I try to pull against him, but he's too strong, and I'm feeling dizzier by the second.

He only tightens his hold on me as he begins dragging me wherever he plans on taking me.

"Stop!" I try to screech, but my voice comes out faint even to my own ears.

Suddenly, a voice cracks through the air like a whip. "I think you'd better let her go." I know that voice. I'll never forget that voice or how it whispered against my skin that night everything changed for me.

"This is none of your business man," Nick's voice sounds irritated as he continues yanking me.

Brad steps from the shadows and towers over him, and Nick releases me before saying, "Jesus, man, whatever," before taking off.

I barely make out Brad's shape before everything starts spinning, and then blackness engulfs me.

Poppy

When I wake up, I sit up groggily, looking around at the unfamiliar space. I'm in a huge bed in an expensive-looking home complete with crown molding and heavy furniture. The events of the night before come rushing back to me, and my heart begins to race.

Me getting dizzy. Nick trying to drag me off somewhere. Brad showing up in the nick of time to save me.

Brad.

I glance down at myself.

"You've still got your clothes on," Brad's voice comes from the corner, and I jump, glancing over to where he sits in a chair watching me. "Unlike that little motherfucker you were with, I'd never take a woman without her consent." His voice is laced with anger. I know what he says is true, though. Hadn't he given me a choice? He'd offered me a way out. He hadn't taken my virginity until I'd consented to it.

I shudder to think of what could have happened if he hadn't shown up when he did.

"Christ," he swears as he stands up and walks over to where I'm still sitting on his bed. "What where you thinking going out dressed like that? And didn't anyone ever tell you not to accept drinks from strangers? It's too easy for fucks like that to spike them."

"You think he spiked my drink?" I ask.

"I know he did," his voice is angry. "You had all the classic symptoms of being drugged."

Seeing as how my head is killing me and I hadn't even drank the whole cup of punch, I have to admit Brad is probably right.

"Where am I?" I ask him.

"My place," he answers simply.

"May I use your bathroom?" I ask him, suddenly becoming aware of my bladder.

He jerks his head to the right. "It's right there."

"Thank you," I mumble as I get up and head over to it. I take care of my business and then brush my teeth as best I can with my finger before splashing water over my face to remove the makeup that makes my eyes look like a raccoon. Courtesy of Melissa's makeover last night.

When I come out of the bathroom, Brad is sitting on the edge of the bed waiting for me. He's just as gorgeous as ever, but for once he's wearing a pair of dark sweatpants and a white shirt instead of his typical khakis or slacks. His muscles are bulging underneath his shirt, and I'm having trouble breathing evenly.

Feeling awkward, I start to thank him, "Thank you for rescuing me last night."

His eyes continue to stare at me intently, and he's still frowning.

"How did you—how were you there?" I ask him. He'd come out of nowhere like some type of avenging angel.

"I was making sure you were safe," he answers before scowling. "Just like I thought, you weren't. Why'd you go to that fucking frat party anyway?" His eyes are blazing now.

I ignore his question and throw back one of my own, "You were following me?"

"You better be glad I was, sweetheart," he says back, shaking his head.

I know he's right, but still. I'm shocked to find out he was following me.

"How long have you been following me?" I ask.

He doesn't answer.

"That long?" I ask incredulously.

"You didn't think I was going to let you slip away again, did you? Not after those weeks of hell I spent searching for you," he tells me frankly, his jaw set stubbornly.

I know I should be angry that he's been following me all this time, and part of me is, but another part of me is flattered that he'd take the time to do that.

Still, it doesn't change anything.

"I need to get back to the dorm," I tell him. "Can I borrow your phone?" I didn't take my phone or purse or anything with me to the party last night.

Brad stands and walks over to me. My heart is beating faster, and my head tilts back to look up at him as he advances. "Why do you need to get going?" he asks me. "I know you don't have any classes on Saturday."

"Because I—I—," I trip over my words, "you're my professor. This isn't right. I can't be here in your home with you. You could get fired."

"Is that why you've been avoiding me?" he asks.

"I haven't been—" I begin.

"Liar," he whispers. "You try to be the first one out of the door every time class is dismissed."

His face is mere inches from mine, his blue eyes piercing me, demanding the truth.

When I don't answer, he sighs brokenly. "I'm sorry, Poppy."

"For what?" I ask in surprise. He's done nothing to be sorry for.

His face looks anguished as he answers, "For letting you sell yourself to me. I had no intention of fulfilling my buddies' "gift," but then I saw you and I couldn't resist you."

I look down at the reminder of what I did, tears

pricking my eyes at his admission that he's sorry, that he regrets what we did.

"I'm sorry you regret it." My voice wobbles, and I feel a few tears slipping from my eyes.

He lifts my chin up and makes me meet his gaze. "That's not what I said, Poppy," He gives a humorless laugh. "Jesus, I don't regret what we did. I just wish I hadn't blown my shot with you. You deserved so much better. If I'd been a gentleman, I'd have made sure you got paid anyway and sent you on your way. I wouldn't have taken advantage of your circumstances. As it is, I'm a selfish prick, and now you can't stand to be near me. I'm sorry if I hurt you."

I shake my head. "That's not it at all," I tell him. "And you did give me a choice, remember?"

He's looking down at me, waiting for an explanation.

I take a deep breath before confessing, "I loved everything we did that night. I can't get it out of my head."

His breathing becomes ragged, and a fire blazes in his eyes.

"Jesus, Poppy. Don't say shit like that unless you're sure you mean it."

"I dream about it every night," I whisper, confessing more.

That confession seems to break him because he hauls me against him and crashes his lips to mine, kissing me like a starving man.

My hands reach up to wrap around his neck, and I'm kissing him back just as passionately.

The way our tongues twine together communicate weeks of longing. His hands move down my back, pulling me closer to him. I feel his hard length against my tummy, and an answering wetness pools between my thighs. I'm throbbing and aching, and I know the only thing that will take it away is being filled by him.

Right now, I don't care if I'll be his secret. I just want him to hold me and make me feel special the way only he can.

So when he suddenly reaches down, grabs my legs, and hoists me up into his arms, my legs automatically wrapping around his waist, I make no move to stop him.

Chapter Five

Brad

I want to eat her up.

Hearing her admit she liked it, that she dreams about it.

Fuuuck.

I can't contain myself. I've been dying to touch her for weeks.

I press her up against the wall, desperate to be inside her.

The tip of my cock is leaking, and I reach down with one hand to release it from my sweatpants. I moan as it pops free, hitting her bare thigh.

Then, I yank her skirt up, not that it has far to go. The flimsy little thing is so damn short. "I ought to spank your ass for leaving your dorm dressed like that," I tell her.

She whimpers, and I run my fingers along her slit.

She's fucking soaked. I feel a jet of precum shoot from my cock at the knowledge.

"Fuck, I've got to get inside you now, baby," I tell her.

She nods, agreeing with me, thank fuck.

That's all the encouragement I need. I pull her thong to the side, and then I push up into her in one hard thrust. She's so wet, I slide right to the hilt.

She screams, and I capture her lips with mine, trying desperately not to come yet. "*This*. This pussy that I've been aching for ever since that first time," I breath against her before I kiss her lips again. I move to kiss her cheeks, her neck, every bit of her face, until I feel the storm within my balls passing.

Her little cunt is gripping me so tight, and I know I won't last long. But I want to see her come. I want to feel her fall apart in my arms.

Holding her perfect little ass up with one hand, I reach between us with the other one and rub my thumb over her clit as I begin to saw in and out of her.

He breath catches, and her eyes close as she moans.

"Open your eyes, baby," I tell her. "I want to see you when you come all over my dick."

She obeys, her brown eyes looking at me dazedly. "Brad, please," she begs, and I almost blow right then at the sound of her saying my name.

I pick up the pace, stroking in and out of her faster, my thumb moving faster on her clit.

Her moans are getting louder, and I can feel my own end nearing. My cock is getting harder, and I feel my balls churning again.

There's no way I'm going to be able to hold back now.

"Come for me, Poppy," I order her, slamming into her harder and faster.

I press down on her clit one last time, and she shatters in my arms, screaming her release, and I've never seen something so beautiful as when she breaks.

I feel her pussy convulsing around me, and that does me in. I release my spend in a roar, the cum tearing from balls and through the stalk of my cock with such intensity my knees go weak.

I keep coming, spurt after spurt as I continue to press into her until it's dripping down her thighs and onto the floor.

She's quivering in my arms as I kiss her gently. I don't want to let her go, so with my cock still inside her, I walk us over to the bed where I finally pull out of her and lay her down.

I lay down beside her and pull her into my arms. We're both still dressed, but that's not the point. I want to hold her.

I kiss her forehead and her eyes before making my way down to her cheeks and chin and finally her lips.

When I stop kissing her, I reach out to stroke her hair. "You're so beautiful, sweetheart." I could stare at her all day. I trace my hand over her shoulder, down her arm, and then over the swell of her hips, memorizing each curve of her body.

"What are we doing here, Brad?" she asks when she finally speaks.

"Making up for lost time," I tell her with a grin before my hand skims over her thigh.

She shakes her head, sitting up in the bed. "No, I mean…that was amazing and everything, but it doesn't change anything."

I wait for her to say more and when she doesn't, I stiffen. "Is there someone else?" I growl, the thought making me want to tear whoever it is limb from limb. I honestly don't think there is. In all my time watching her, I've never seen her with another guy except last night when she went to that frat party. My blood boils again just thinking of the danger she put herself in.

She shakes her head, "No, it's not that at all."

I relax, but I frown at her. "You're running from me again. I can already see it."

She stands from the bed, putting distance between us. "You're still my professor. I'm still your student, and this still can't happen."

I clench my jaw. "Don't tell me you don't want this because you confessed that you do."

She sighs in exasperation. "It doesn't matter what I want. It is what it is. You could lose your job, Brad." Her eyes are sad as she looks at me, worried for me, and I feel something soften inside me.

"Fuck my job," I tell her honestly.

Her eyes widen. "You don't mean that," she says.

"I sure as fuck do. You're more important than that. I can always find another job if I get fired."

She just shakes her head sadly again. "I couldn't ask you to do that. Besides, it's not just that. If we start seeing each other, then what will that do to me? People will begin to question my grades in your class. I don't want my entire academic reputation ruined before I've even gotten one. I've worked too hard to get here, Brad. Doing well in college is important to me," she admits, her eyes pleading with me to understand.

I look at her, disgruntled because I know what she says is true. It's not just my job on the line but her reputation as well. While I don't care about my job, I don't want her reputation ruined.

"What do you suggest we do then?" I ask her quietly, already knowing her answer.

"I think we need to just," she stumbles over her words before she lifts her chin, "just not see each other anymore."

I give a harsh laugh. "Yeah, not going to fucking happen, Poppy." I stand up from the bed now and stalk toward her, noting how she takes a step back for every step I take toward her.

I keep stalking toward her until her back is pressed against the wall again, and then I frown down at her and tell her frankly, "You can't tell me you loved what we did and that you've been dreaming about it every night and then expect me to just turn my back on what we have like it never existed."

"You have to," she whispers.

I run my finger along the column of her throat, lowering my face to hers, intending to kiss her until she changes her mind, but she holds up her hands and says, "Don't, please."

I pull back. It's like she's gutted me with those words. I know she wants this as much as I do, but she's too damn stubborn and noble for either of our good.

"You're fucking killing me here, Poppy," I tell her.

"Please, just let me call a cab."

"No," I tell her immediately.

Her brow furrows, and a hint of worry creeps into her eyes. It pisses me off to no end. She must know I'd never hurt her or keep her here against her will.

Of course, I did basically confess to stalking her, so maybe she's justified in not knowing that. *Fuck.*

I study her for a moment before I turn and grab my keys off my dresser. "If you want to go, I'll drive you. At least that way I know you'll get there safely."

She visibly exhales in relief, and it's like a knife to my heart.

But what can I do?

So I drive her back to her dorm, even though ever fiber of my being is screaming for me not to.

***

Poppy

Brad didn't speak a word the whole way to my dorm. He sat behind the wheel of his black Audi with his jaw clenched, his hands so tight on the wheel his knuckles were white.

He's angry. I get that, but surely he can see this is how it has to be.

I should have kept myself under control. I shouldn't have confessed all that to him, but at that moment when he'd been looming above me, apologizing for that night, I'd wanted nothing more than to be in his arms again. I didn't want him to regret it. I didn't want him to regret us—even if there could be no us.

He grabs my hand before I can get out of the car, kissing my palm with his blue eyes riveted on me the entire time.

"This isn't over, Poppy," he tells me as I get out of his car.

I don't say anything.

But I know what I have to do now.

He's not going to let it go, and I din't want him to risk getting fired, so I have to remove the temptation.

I haven't been to class in a week.

I've been following the syllabus and turning in assignments through the virtual classroom.

I miss seeing his face, though. I miss the intensity

of his eyes, but being in the same vicinity with him is dangerous—to both of us.

He made it clear he doesn't care about propriety, so I'm the one who has to. He might say he doesn't mind losing his job to be with me, but I'm not so convinced. Brad obviously loves what he does. I can't allow him to sacrifice that for me.

I sigh and log into my art class where I submit assignments. There's a notification flashing in the upper right corner of the screen, and I click on it, eager to see my grade on my latest paper.

I stare at the screen stupidly for a few moments, not quite comprehending what I'm seeing.

A *D*. The bastard gave me a *D*.

I've been getting *A*'s all semester. I know I know my stuff when it comes to art. This paper was my best work yet. I poured my heart and soul into it. Just because I can't physically go to art class because of my too-tempting art professor doesn't mean that I'm not still as passionate about art as ever and that I don't crave his approval as a teacher.

I scan the file for any comments on what I did wrong, what he didn't like.

There are none.

No explanation for this *D* that would drag my grade down.

No, he didn't failed me, but he gave me as close as he could to a failing grade.

I ball my hands up into fists and fume, glaring at the computer screen.

This is unacceptable! He gives me a horrible grade and leaves *no* comments about it. None whatsoever?

I print my graded paper out, slap my laptop shut, and head out the door, one destination in mind.

I know Brad doesn't have any classes now, so I stomp right into his room and back to his office. The door is open, so I march right in.

He sits back in his desk as I enter, but I notice he doesn't look the least bit surprised to see me.

"What the hell is this?" I ask as I fling my paper onto his desk, livid.

His eyes don't even look at the paper I've flung at him. He already knows what I'm talking about.

"Miss Montgomery," his deep voice comes out like a taunting caress, "To what do I owe this pleasure?"

"Cut the crap, *Professor* Davenport," I stress 'professor,' and his eyes flare in irritation. "My paper was good. I know it was. It doesn't deserve this grade, and you left no feedback on why you gave it to me."

He grins at me, an infuriating, beautifully devastating grin. "It worked, didn't it?"

I stare at him like an idiot before it all clicks into place. He knew the bad grade would piss me off and get me to come see him, effectively making me break my rule of keeping distance between us. The asshole.

I stand there like a deer caught in the headlights for a moment, trying to decide where to run. His eyes are trained on me fiercely, like a predator stalking its prey, his muscles tense as if he's ready to pounce.

As soon as I take one step back, he's up and around the desk so fast I'm surprised he didn't turn his chair over.

The next thing I know I'm pressed flush against him, and his lips crash onto mine.

He kisses me roughly, letting all his pent-up frustration come through in his kisses. I feel like he's going to devour me with his heat. "You can't run away from this, Poppy," he rasps against my lips.

I feel his hardness pressing into me, and I moan, the sensitive flesh between my thighs suddenly hot and achy, all thoughts of keeping my distance from him gone.

Someone clears their throat behind us, and I still, mortified.

The door is still standing wide open, and I pull

away from Brad and turn to see who it is, but he doesn't let me get far. He pulls me up against his side, wrapping his arm around me protectively.

It's the dean of the fucking university, and he's frowning at us. Oh god, Brad is going to lose his job.

"Well, I see why you sent me that sudden resignation this morning," the dean says, his eyes still flicking between us. "I was hoping I could talk you out of it, but I see now that's not an option…" he trails off.

Resignation? I glance up at Brad, and he looks down at me. "You gave up your job?" I ask him weakly.

"You were so worried about me getting fired you wouldn't see me, so I quit. Problem solved."

The dean clears his voice again before asking sternly, "How long has this been going on? You know you can't give students preferential treatment because you're in a, uh," he stumbles, "a relationship, don't you, Davenport?"

Brad reaches onto his desk to pick up the paper he gave me a *D* on. He hands the paper to the dean, saying, "As you can see, she's definitely gotten no preferential treatment."

The dean glances down at the paper and then nods curtly as if that puts his mind at ease. "Well, in that case, we'll keep this little, uh, display," he motions to us, "just between us. Davenport," he speaks directly to Brad now, "you've left us in a bit of a pickle, but seeing as how you've found a replacement to cover your class for the rest of the semester, I guess we can't be too upset about this impromptu resignation."

Brad just nods, and then the dean stands there uncertainly for a moment before he shoves his hands in his pockets and leaves, closing the door behind him.

The tears I've been holding in finally slip free, "But, Brad, you love teaching art." I look up at him guiltily, not believing he gave up his job for me.

He wipes them from my cheeks before telling me, "And I still will. I can teach anywhere. I don't have to be a member of university staff to teach. The question is," his voice becomes gravelly, "are you going to stop fucking running from me now and let me love you?"

I look up at him, this gorgeous man with his dark hair and piercing blue eyes that seem to see right into my soul. Then, I realize just what he said, and my eyes widen.

He chuckles and answers my unspoken question, "Yes, Poppy Montgomery, I love you. You've been driving me insane for weeks. You're all I can fucking think about." His voice drops an octave. "You've been mine since that first night. You know it too."

I feel a shiver go up my spine. Yes, I do. I haven't been able to forget him no matter how much I've tried. He's owned me since that first night I gave myself to him.

"I love you too, Brad," I confess, and I do. It may have happened impossibly fast, but I know deep down inside me that I do. I do love him, and I'm tired of fighting it. I want to be with him. So we didn't meet the most conventional way. Brad doesn't care, and neither do I. If I hadn't made that hard decision to sell my virginity, I might never have met him. So, to hell with what the world may think.

"Fuck, sweetheart," he groans before he kisses me again, lifting me up into his arms and pulling my legs to wrap around his waist. His thick length is pulsing against me through our clothes, and I writhe on him wantonly.

His eyes darken, and he swipes everything off his desk with one hand, the other still holding me against him securely.

He pulls my dress up as he bends me over his desk. "If you only knew how many times I wanted to drag you in here after class and fuck the living daylights out of you," he growls before sinking into me in one hard thrust.

I cry out, instantly shaking, on the verge of shattering. He feels even bigger from this angle, and he's pounding me relentlessly.

"This isn't fucking, Poppy," he tells me. "This is mating. I'm claiming you as mine, just like I claimed you that first night when that virginal little pussy creamed all over me for the first time. I'm the only one who's ever going to be inside you this way. Your first and your last. This pussy is mine. Do you understand me?"

His possessive words are bringing me closer to the brink of ecstasy, and all I can do is moan and pant, the ticklish sensation between my legs growing more intense with each word he speaks and every give of his hips.

He leans over my back, his huge arms on other side of me and kisses my shoulder, licking and biting on my skin, before he grabs a fistful of my hair and slams into me again, hitting that delicious spot inside me, and then I'm screaming as my muscles contract and pulse around him.

He roars like a lion, "*Mine*! Goddammit, you're mine, Poppy!" He moans raggedly as he floods me with splash after splash of his liquid heat. I feel his spend jet deep within me as his hard length pulses inside me, pushing me off the edge again as I orgasm a second time, coming with him.

He collapses on my back, his heavy weight pressing into me as he pushes my hair aside and softly kisses the nape of my neck.

"So, professor," I ask him coyly when he finally turns me over and sits me up on his desk to gather me against his chest. "What grade do I get?"

"An *A* fucking plus," he growls, "but on one condition." He looks down at me seriously before continuing, "No more fucking frat parties, and you come home to me from now on."

I laugh and readily agree, "Done, but only if you'll teach me everything you know."

His eyes are like blue flames as he says, "Give me your undivided attention, and there's much I'll teach you, my eager little student."

And then he kisses me, his kiss filled with promise. A promise that I'm finally willing to accept.

Five Years Later

Brad

I watch my wife as she sashays toward me, her slightly protruding belly filling me with a sense of pride.

Mine.

She's always been mine ever since that first night I claimed her, but fuck me if I don't get off on seeing her swell with my child, a message to all the world who she belongs to.

"You look beautiful, sweetheart," I tell her, planting a kiss on her forehead as she reaches me.

She smiles up at me with that trusting look of innocence that makes me surge with possessiveness.

Thank God she doesn't mind my possessiveness because it's only gotten worse since she agreed to marry me.

We waited until after she finished college. She graduated at the top of her class, of course. No surprise there. My wife is intelligent, and her paintings are actually really good. Not that I'm surprised. I'm not. I always knew she had talent.

I've continued teaching just like I told her, but instead of teaching at the university, I've set up my own studio where I teach sculpting master classes. I actually enjoy this better than teaching at the university because I can play by my own rules this way and focus on what I truly love: sculpting.

I've also taken up sculpting just for pleasure again. Unsurprisingly, Poppy is my muse.

I take her hand and lead her into my studio that is filled with sculptures of her beautiful face, hands, and in a private section in the back of the studio, her body. I don't leave those sculptures of her body on display, though, too jealous to even entertain the thought of anyone else getting to see her how I do, art be damned. Those are for our eyes only.

Poppy has a studio right next to mine where she

paints. She sells a lot of her pieces to art galleries, and I sell many of my sculptures too, but what the curators love the most are our collaborations.

They were purely Poppy's idea. She wanted to paint one of my sculptures one day, and while I'd eyed her dubiously, I'd of course let her do it. She can have anything she fucking wants from me. All she has to do was ask. If she asks me to give her the sun, I'll do my damnedest to try to find a way to lasso the fucker and drag it down from the sky.

Anyway, turns out my sculptures with her feathery, impressionist scenes painted on them are the new avant garde. They're all the rage, so much so that we receive so many commissions we have to decline many of them, especially now that she's pregnant.

I frown at her as she picks up a brush and deftly pluck it from her fingertips. "No working tonight, sweetheart. I don't want you overdoing it in your condition."

She pouts and scoffs at the same time, "Brad, I'm fine. This sculpture still needs to be painted, and I feel okay. I promise I won't overdo it. Besides, I'm barely showing."

It's true. She's barely in her second trimester, but I know Poppy's determination and work ethic. She'll overdo it if I let her.

She balls her hands into little fists at her sides when I don't give her the brush back, and I chuckle. She looks like an angry kitten with its back raised. Harmless yet feisty. "You're cute when you're angry, baby."

She opens her mouth to fire back some smart ass retort I'm sure, but I lean in and kiss her, silencing her protest. She melts against me despite herself, and I chuckle again. I love the way she becomes pliant in my arms, her body molding to mine so perfectly.

I hoist her up onto my work table and take my time with her, kissing down the column of her throat and over her breasts, running my hands along the gentle swell of her belly before dropping little kisses there.

I mean what I said. I don't want her overdoing it when she's pregnant, and that goes for sexually too. Ever since I found out she's expecting I've been extra gentle with her, frustratingly so to her sometimes. I've been making love to her slow and easy, cherishing her —the way she should have had it the first time. There'll be plenty of time for rough fucking and mating later.

She looks down at me lovingly, and I go back up to claim her mouth again before I unleash myself from my pants and slide slowly into her.

She gasps and clenches around me. I'm so fucking hard I could bust already. She never fails to do me that way. It doesn't matter how many times I've had her. It's never enough. She's my obsession, and I'd live inside her if I could.

I stroke her slowly, eliciting sweet sighs and moans from her lips while I kiss and caress every inch of her, molding my hands over her soft body, loving the feel of her skin underneath my fingertips more than any clay.

My blood is thrumming in my veins, and I feel the tell-tale sign of my balls clenching up. I know I won't last long, but I need to feel her fall apart. I latch onto one of her nipples and reach between us to stroke her clit while I pump into her a couple more times, painstakingly slow but enough to send waves of pleasure rushing up to my tip.

"Brad," she whines my name, and it's like music to my ears. There's no sweeter sound than the sound of my name dripping from her lips when she's about to come.

"Come on, baby. I've got you," I tell her, pressing down harder on her clit, and then I feel it. Her pussy pulses and grips, molding around me, and I release into her with a strangled croak, painting the inside of her womb with my spend. She might be the painter and me the sculpter, but when our bodies are joined, she's the one sculpting me and I'm the one painting her.

My arms are shaking, and I feel her legs quivering underneath me as we both catch our breath after the intensity of our orgasms. It doesn't matter if we fuck fast or make love slow, we're always like this afterward, spent after our intense climaxes.

"Of all the ways we sculpt and paint together, this is by far my favorite," I tell her.

She laughs, and my lips tip up at the sound.

"How'd I do, sweetheart?" I ask her, rubbing my nose against her.

"*A* fucking plus," she grades me before giggling as I laugh, thanking whatever fate brought us together.

THE END

Connect with Emma!

Visit Emma's website to get a **FREE** book you can't get anywhere else: www.authoremmabray.com.

www.ingramcontent.com/pod-product-compliance
Lightning Source LLC
Chambersburg PA
CBHW021039160726
47994CB00006B/2638